AZTEC TIMES

Written by
Antony Mason

SIMON & SCHUSTER BOOKS FOR YOUNG READERS

CONTENTS

INTRODUCTION

In 1519 a band of 600 Spanish soldiers led by Hernán Cortés landed in their sailing ships on the east coast of Mexico. They were venturing into new lands, never before visited by Europeans. After marching 400 miles from the coast, they reached Tenochtitlán, the Aztec capital. Built on islands on a lake, it was larger than any European city of the time—and every bit as magnificent.

The Aztecs were rulers of an empire stretching across most of central Mexico. They had been in power for less than 100 years, the latest of a long series of great civilizations that had risen and fallen in this region over nearly 3,000 years. The Spanish were amazed. The Aztecs had towering temples, vast markets trading in all kinds of goods, bands of splendid warriors, nobles glittering with gold jewelry. But their religion also demanded cruel human sacrifice, which horrified the Spanish. Within just two years, Cortés had conquered and destroyed Tenochtitlán and the Aztec empire quickly crumbled. Before long the Aztec civilization had virtually disappeared.

**A carving of
Huehueteotl, the
fire god**

ORIGINS

The early American civilizations started developing in Mexico and Central America. The first was created by the Olmecs about 3,000 years ago, closely followed by the Maya. The Maya flourished between A.D. 250 and 900, and became the greatest of these early American civilizations.

In the 500s Teotihuacán in central Mexico became a very powerful city-state, but 250 years later it was mysteriously abandoned—the strange fate of many of the ancient cities of this region. Later the war-like Toltecs ruled central Mexico from their capital at Tula, until about 1200.

Around 1428 a new people began to dominate central Mexico. They called themselves the Mexica—but we know them as the Aztecs.

▼The ball game, known as tlachtli *or* pot-a-tok, *was played by most of the Meso-American civilizations. The rules are not known for sure, but it seems that two teams of players knocked the ball around the court using their hips, elbows, and knees. The stone rings found at some courts were probably used as goals.*

Spectators gambled heavily on the result of a game. Stories tell of wealthy noblemen losing everything they possessed by gambling at ball games.

Players wore feathered hats and padded knee, hip, and elbow protectors.

The Olmecs

Occupying the fertile coastal region of eastern Mexico, the Olmecs developed a sophisticated civilization that lasted from about 1200 to 400 B.C. They built the earliest temple pyramids and introduced number systems and picture writing. Although they only had stone tools, they made superb carvings out of jade, a hard, green stone. Their most extraordinary monuments, however, are the vast stone heads carved out of basalt. Of the sixteen heads found, the largest was eleven feet tall.

Meso-America

Meso-America, meaning "Middle America," is a term used to describe the lands of Central America and Mexico. The ancient civilizations that developed in this area shared several common features. They all built temple pyramids, used picture writing, believed in many of the same gods, and carried out the practice of human (and sometimes animal) sacrifice. Maize (corn) was widely farmed in the region, and was vital to the subsistence of all the different Meso-American peoples.

The rectangular courts often formed part of temple complexes, an indication that the game was played as part of religious ceremonies.

The Zapotecs and Mixtecs

The Zapotecs lived in the Oaxaca Valley. Their civilization developed after A.D. 300 and lasted until about 950. This was also the greatest period of the Mayan civilization, which lay to their east. The Zapotecs built their capital city and religious center at Monte Albán, with palaces, temples, and homes spread over a huge area. This was eventually abandoned and taken over by their neighbors, the Mixtecs. Like the Zapotecs, the Mixtecs produced beautiful artifacts in pottery, stone, and metal. Wars between the Zapotecs and the Mixtecs lasted for several centuries, until they joined forces to face a new enemy: the Aztecs.

Zapotec gold figure

The ball was made of solid rubber taken from the sap of rubber trees.

▶*Palenque, the westernmost Mayan city, was mysteriously abandoned in about A.D. 900, along with the other Mayan cities. With the help of the Toltecs, however, some Mayan cities revived elsewhere—for instance at Chichén Itzá—and the Mayan civilization survived throughout the Aztec period. But at Palenque the jungle took over. It was not until 1746 that the ruins were discovered. This temple (right) housed the funeral chamber of a Mayan lord.*

7

RULERS OF THE VALLEY

According to their legends, the Aztecs left Aztlán (in the north of Meso-America) in about 1125 and began 200 years of wandering. They were led by their tribal god Huitzilopochtli, who promised them a new land in a place where an eagle would be seen on a cactus, eating a serpent.

The Aztecs first settled near Tula. Later they traveled through the Valley of Mexico and settled on the shores of Lake Texcoco. In about 1325 they were forced to take refuge on a swampy island on the lake where apparently an eagle on a cactus had been seen. Here they founded the great city of Tenochtitlán. By the mid-1400s the Aztecs were the most powerful people in the region, having defeated other warring tribes.

The eagle on the cactus

▲ *Mexico City, the modern capital of Mexico, is built over the site of Tenochtitlán. Little of the Aztec city has survived, but the volcano of Popocatépetl still rises over the valley.*

Heavy loads were carried in bags and baskets, supported by a strap that looped around the forehead.

Thousands of workmen were needed to build the city of Tenochtitlán. Some were skilled craftsmen, but the heavy work was done by prisoners of war and laborers sent from neighboring states ruled by the Aztecs.

The great temple

The first thing that the Aztecs did when they arrived on their island was to build a temple to their gods Huitzilopochtli, god of war and the sun, and Tlaloc, the rain god. Eventually they produced a magnificent step-pyramid. When it was completed in 1487 it was about 200 feet high. It had two shrines on the top: a red one for Huitzilopochtli, and a blue one for Tlaloc.

Tenochtitlán

From its beginnings on a swampy island, Tenochtitlán grew into a magnificent city of 250,000 people. The Aztecs named their capital city after the chieftain who had led them there, Tenoch, and the word for a cactus, *nochtli*. The land was drained by building canals which criss-crossed the city. Three roads across the water, called causeways, and an aqueduct carrying fresh water, linked the city to the mainland.

All the stone had to be brought from quarries on the mainland by boat. Large blocks were dragged to the building site on log rollers.

The stone was covered in plaster and painted in bright colors.

NEZAHUALCÓYOTL

Texcoco, to the east of the lake, was a city of 45,000 people. From 1431 to 1472 it was ruled by its greatest tlatoani (leader), Nezahualcóyotl, a powerful warrior. He helped form an alliance with the Aztecs, to fight and defeat the Tepanecs. Under Nezahualcóyotl's rule, Texcoco became a famous center for learning and culture. Nezahualcóyotl himself was a celebrated builder, law-maker, and poet. He also kept a large zoo. Nezahualcóyotl was so revered by his people that they thought he was descended from the gods. At the same time, the Aztecs were ruled by a great tlatoani called Motecuhzoma I (1440–68). He was later called Montezuma I by the Spanish.

To cut and shape stone, the Aztecs used tools made of a very hard volcanic stone called obsidian.

◄*The Great Temple, at the center of Tenochtitlán, was rebuilt at least four times before its completion in 1487. Each time, the earlier pyramids were covered over as the temple became larger and more magnificent. The tops of earlier pyramids formed rooms inside the final pyramid, and these were used as inner temples.*

THE DEMANDS OF THE GODS

Xipe Totec, wearing a flayed human skin

The Aztecs held a four-day opening ceremony of the Great Temple of Tenochtitlán in 1487. According to some reports, 80,000 people were sacrificed to the gods. The Aztecs lived in a cruel world, ruled by demanding gods. They believed that they had to make regular sacrifices to the gods—of animals or people— to ensure that it would rain, and that their crops would produce enough food. They thought that the gods themselves needed blood to survive. If Huitzilopochtli, the sun god, did not receive blood he would die, and the sun would disappear. If Tlaloc, the rain god, became displeased, he would punish the Aztecs with drought or floods. In other words, unless sacrifices were performed daily, disaster would follow.

▲ *The evil Coyolxauhqui, sister of the Aztec war god*

Huehueteotl

Xiuhtecuhtli

Sacred fire was carefully kept burning in the temples as a symbol of continuing life.

The victim was led up the temple steps, then held over the sacrificial stone by the priests. Another priest used a sharp stone knife to make the human sacrifice.

A god for everything

The Aztecs had a god for every aspect of their lives—for children, for maize, for games, for the wind, and so on. The roles of many of the gods overlapped. For instance, Xiuhtecuhtli and Huehueteotl were both gods of fire. Xipe Totec was the god of plants and the springtime. He received a particularly gruesome form of sacrifice: The skin of a victim was removed and worn by a priest, representing the rebirth of plants each spring.

◀ *A sacrificial knife with an obsidian (volcanic rock) blade*

The sacrificial priests did not wash, and never cut their hair. They looked wild and dirty.

Human sacrifice

The Aztec tradition of sacrifice demanded over 10,000 victims a year. Most Aztecs accepted this as normal and necessary. The victims were usually captured criminals, slaves, or prisoners; but they were sometimes normal Aztec men, women, and children. Captured warriors were also sacrificed: They were treated well by their captors, and went to their deaths with pride, thinking that they would be rewarded with a happy afterlife. The captors cooked and ate the arms or legs of the dead victim, believing that they became holy through sacrifice. The skulls of the many victims were displayed in front of the temple on a skull rack. Not all victims were killed by a priest's knife, some were beheaded or drowned.

Warring gods

Tezcatlipoca

Two of the most important gods were constantly at war with each other. Tezcatlipoca represented the dark side of human nature: He controlled the fate of people and was in charge of magic. Quetzalcoatl, the feathered serpent, was the god of nature and knowledge, among other things. According to the myth, Tezcatlipoca eventually won the war by trickery; Quetzalcoatl was disgraced and forced to leave the Toltec lands. He headed east, promising to return one day to reclaim his throne. By some accounts, he prophesied that he would return in the Aztec year called "1 reed:" 1519.

Quetzalcoatl

◀ *The Aztec religion was run by a powerful group of high priests who organized the many festivals and carried out the sacrifices. They were well-educated noblemen, but they led hard lives, often torturing themselves to please the gods. People believed that only these priests could talk to the gods.*

FEEDING THE CITY

Chicomecoatl, the goddess of maize seeds

A big city like Tenochtitlán consumed a large amount of food, so the Aztecs depended on the great skills of their farmers. They grew a wide variety of crops, and kept turkeys, ducks, and a small breed of dog for meat. Fishing provided another valuable source of protein. The Aztecs also enjoyed eating some more unusual things collected from the wild, such as frogs, snails, grasshoppers, and insect eggs.

The Aztecs always lived with the threat of famine. As Tenochtitlán grew, even in good years the land could not produce enough food. This was one reason why the Aztecs began to conquer their neighbors—to control more farming land.

FARMING TOOLS

The Aztecs used very simple tools for farming, usually made of wood and stone, and sometimes of a metal, such as copper. These were good enough for the soft, damp soil of the chinampas. Digging sticks were normally made of wood and could be used for hoeing and planting. Hoes were used for breaking up the soil and weeding between the crops.

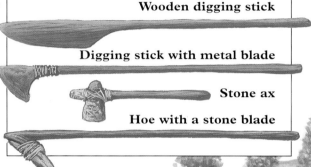

Wooden digging stick

Digging stick with metal blade

Stone ax

Hoe with a stone blade

▶ *Many of the details of daily Aztec life were recorded in illustrated books, called codices, written during Aztec times or immediately afterward. This is a page from a codex showing an Aztec farming scene.*

The chinampas were separated by canals. Harvested crops could be loaded directly into boats and taken across the lake to the city markets.

The soil was kept rich by adding compost and manure—including human excrement collected from Tenochtitlán.

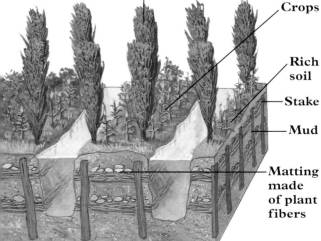

Willow trees

Crops

Rich soil

Stake

Mud

Matting made of plant fibers

Chinampas

Some of the best land around Tenochtitlán was created in the lake itself. The chinampas were gardens built up in long thin strips on the lake bed. First the farmers drove wooden stakes into the mud and joined these with fencing. Then they filled the enclosed area with layers of soil and matting, weighed down by stones. Trees helped to hold down the soil with their roots. Fertilized by dung, these rich "floating gardens" could produce several crops a year.

White maize

Black maize

▲ *Maize (corn) was the most important crop. It was used to make porridge, tamales (cakes), and tortillas (dry maize pancakes). Maize cobs were small, and the kernels were often red or black.*

Growing food

The Aztecs grew a wide variety of vegetables, including sweet potatoes, sweet peppers, beans, chilies, onions, and tomatoes. Other common foods included the fruit from the prickly pear cactus, and the seeds of the amaranth plant, which were made into dough. Cocoa beans were grown in the tropical forests. They were very expensive and were used to make a bitter drink that was considered a real luxury. Many of these foods were unknown in Europe at that time.

▼ *Many of the chinampas were owned by noblemen and rented out to farmers in return for a share in the crops produced. The farmers had to follow official calendars, which told them when to plant and harvest each crop.*

Sweet potato

Cocoa beans

Avocado

Chilies

Squash

Sweet peppers

Vanilla

Peanuts

All farm work was done by hand. The Aztecs did not have any animals, such as horses or oxen, to help them plow the fields.

The chinampas today

The largest group of chinampas was at the southern end of Lake Texcoco, in two areas called Lake Xochimilco and Lake Chalco. Today the only surviving chinampas (below) are in Lake Xochimilco. Once there were 15,000 gardens here; now there are fewer than 1,000, but these have been preserved as a park. Xochimilco means "the place of the fields of flowers," a reminder that the chinampas were also used to grow flowers, which the Aztecs took to decorate their houses and to offer as gifts.

FAMILY LIFE

The Aztecs lived a harsh life, devoted to the gods, in which their daily routines were carefully planned and organized. They were brought up to be obedient, hardworking, and respectful. There was very little crime or bad behavior. Punishments were severe; children who misbehaved might be pinched, spanked, or pricked with cactus spikes.

Families were very important, and most people lived in close contact with a large number of their relatives. All families belonged to a local community organization or clan called a *calpulli*, which had its own temple and schools. Aztecs married in their late teens or early twenties. Parents arranged the marriage—but the couple had some say in the choice.

A pottery figurine of a mother carrying two children

Girls were taught to spin thread from cotton or other plant fibers. The thread was then used to weave cloth.

Thatched roof

Furnace

Bath house

◀ *Most people lived in small, one-room houses built of adobe (mud-brick), or wattle (woven branches) plastered with mud. Country houses usually had roofs made of grass thatch. In the cities, smarter flat-roofed houses were often built of stone and set around a shared courtyard. Almost all houses had a bath house. A fire was lit in the furnace, and water was thrown on the wall of the bath house next door to create steam.*

Walls made of wattle plastered with mud

There was very little furniture inside most homes. People sat and slept on the floor on mats made of woven reeds.

Musical instruments

Families and *calpulli* came together regularly to celebrate births, marriages, religious ceremonies, and great national events such as victories at war. Music, singing, and dancing always played a major part in these festivities. Aztec instruments included flutes, panpipes, trumpets made of conch shells, whistles, rattles, gongs, and drums, but no stringed instruments.

A pottery flute

14

All homes had small shrines to the gods that might help to protect the family.

▲ *It was a woman's job to grind maize into flour to make tortillas and tamales. The maize kernels were placed on a curved slab of volcanic stone and crushed under a kind of rolling pin. Tortillas were the most common food of the Aztecs, and they were freshly made every day.*

Tortillas were baked on a pottery disk, which was placed over the fire on three stones, a symbol of the fire god.

Clay bowls and baskets were used for storing and carrying food.

◄ *Aztec women ran the home, raised children, cooked, and made clothes. Their day began at dawn, and usually ended at sunset, when most people went to bed. The Aztecs believed that evil spirits roamed outside through the night, so few people went out after dark.*

Nobles

Aztec society was ruled by a wealthy and powerful group of nobles. Ordinary people could become nobles, if, for example, they showed great bravery on the battlefield. At the very top was the *tlatoani*, who lived in a magnificent palace. A new *tlatoani* was elected from among the nobles, but usually was a member of the last *tlatoani's* family.

The *tlatoani* traveled about on a litter carried by nobles.

BRINGING UP CHILDREN

Older children went to school, but parents were responsible for most of their children's education. At the age of four a child started to learn work skills and household chores. Codex drawings show children receiving instructions. The blue dots show the age; the tortillas show how much food they should receive. The scrolls next to the mouths indicate who is speaking.

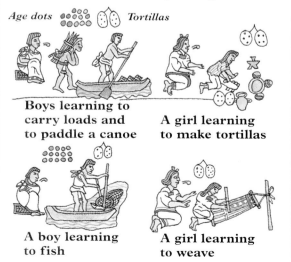

Age dots   *Tortillas*

Boys learning to carry loads and to paddle a canoe

A girl learning to make tortillas

A boy learning to fish

A girl learning to weave

ARTS AND CRAFTS

When the Aztecs came to power, the Meso-Americans had been producing a remarkable range of arts and crafts for over 2,000 years. Products were made for use in daily life, but much of the finest work was done for religious purposes.

Specialist craftworkers were held in high esteem by the Aztecs. They had their own guilds, customs, and gods. Tenochtitlán became a center for their workshops.

To the Aztecs, however, the greatest art of all was poetry, written in their complex language, Nahuatl. Rich, powerful nobles paid singer-poets to compose poetry to celebrate important events—or composed it themselves.

A giant stone sculpture of the serpent-skirt goddess Coatlicue

▼ *Quetzals live in the high rain forests of Central America. The bright green and crimson feathers from the male quetzal were the most valuable of all feathers to the Aztecs.*

Large feathers were carefully trimmed. Then, to hold them in place on a fan or headdress, the quills were fixed into a bamboo tube before being sewn onto the frame.

Some ordinary feathers, such as turkey or duck, were sometimes dyed with bright colors to make them look more exciting.

Aztec pottery

Aztec pots had a practical use: They were used to store and carry things, or to help in the preparation or presentation of food. Pots were made by hand, and without a potter's wheel. Round pots were made by building up coils of clay and smoothing down the sides. They were fired in kilns at low temperatures to make the clay hard. Since glaze had not been discovered, pots were decorated with mineral colors, often in zigzags or stepped patterns, or with pictures of plants or animals.

16

PRECIOUS STONES

The Aztecs were particularly fond of stones such as jade, obsidian, and onyx. Jade, a deep-green stone, was considered sacred: It had twice the value of gold. Pieces of the blue-green stone turquoise, as well as red coral and shells, were used to create mosaic-like patterns on masks and other objects.

Jade lip plug

Monkey-shaped obsidian pot

Obsidian grasshopper

Necklace

Turquoise mosaic mask

Like many professional craft workers, feather workers carried out their trade in small family groups, with both husband and wife, and their children contributing to the work. They were also members of a feather workers' guild—an association designed to protect their trade.

Gold mask

▲*Throughout the Aztec period, the greatest goldworkers were the Mixtecs. Some of them worked in Tenochtitlán. The gold was found in riverbeds. It was cast in molds or beaten into shape with hammers.*

Weaving

Weaving was a woman's task, learned from the age of fourteen. The Aztecs used backstrap looms: The vertical threads on the loom were held taut by a strap fixed around the weaver's back. Quality cloth was made from cotton, but most people wore a rougher kind of cloth made from the fibers of the cactus-like maguey (or agave) plant. The dyes used to color cloth were made from plants or animal products, such as bright red cochineal which came from an insect.

▶ *In modern Mexico, dancers at a festival in Cuetzalan, to the east of Mexico City, still wear huge headdresses decorated with feathers—a reminder of the feather headdresses worn by their Aztec ancestors five hundred years ago.*

CLOTHES AND ORNAMENTS

Aztec clothes were simple but comfortable. The men wore a loin cloth, which went around the waist and between the legs and was tied at the front. This is all that they wore when working in the fields, but in cool weather, and at ceremonies, they wore a cloak tied at the shoulder. Women generally wore a simple skirt and tunic top. Most people's clothes were made of the rough maguey fiber. The more expensive cotton cloth was worn only by wealthy people.

Children wore small versions of adult clothes

Ordinary people usually wore white clothes with the edges decorated by embroidery or patterns of dyed thread. Nobles, officials, priests, and high-ranking warriors followed the same style, but their clothes were brilliantly colorful. Noblemen wore cloaks covered with imaginative designs, which included complex patterns and images of birds, butterflies, and shells. They adorned themselves with elaborate jewelry, and at ceremonies they wore huge feather headdresses.

Montezuma's headdress

The *tlatoani* was the most splendidly dressed of all nobles. A magnificent headdress (below) made of quetzal feathers and blue cotinga feathers, of the sort worn by *tlatoani*, still exists in a museum in Vienna, Austria. This was given by Motecuhzoma Xocoyotzin (Montezuma II) to the Spanish conquistador Hernán Cortés, who in turn gave it to his king, Charles V. Some say that it is Montezuma's crown; others say that it was the headdress of an Aztec priest. In either case, it gives an idea of the splendor of Aztec ceremonial clothing.

▼*Many of the jewels, feathers, and cloak designs worn by noblemen were emblems of rank, power, and sacred links with the gods. Laws, punishable by death if disobeyed, prevented ordinary people from wearing clothes or ornaments belonging to senior ranks.*

Only the nobles wore shoes of any kind. Their sandals were often elaborately decorated with gold and jewels, or made from the precious hide of wild animals, such as jaguars. —

Women's clothes

Women wore a long, wrap-around skirt, held up at the waist by a woven belt. In the country many women wore no top at all, but noblewomen and women in the city wore a tunic-like blouse. The clothes of noblewomen could be as magnificent as the men's, with brightly colored patterns, embroidery, and fringes.

Noblewomen took great trouble about their appearance. To make themselves more beautiful, they used an ointment to give their skin a slightly yellow color, and some even stained their teeth black.

Aztec men had smooth-skinned faces and barely needed to shave. Sometimes in later life they grew long, wispy beards.

Nobles added to the dazzling effect of their clothes by carrying bunches of fresh flowers and fans made of brightly colored feathers.

Jewelry

Both men and women wore jewelry—armbands, earrings, and necklaces—and the higher their rank in society, the more they could wear. Noblemen also wore golden crownlike decorations on their foreheads. Some of this jewelry was huge, like the double-headed serpent button (below), which was probably worn across the chest.

STATUS SYMBOLS

Hairstyles signified people's rank or status. Ordinary men had their hair cut in a fringe, but warriors tied their hair up in a topknot. Married women tied their hair up into two hornlike bundles, while unmarried girls let their hair flow free. Another status symbol was a plug which only high-ranking noblemen were allowed to wear through their nose or through the flesh beneath the lower lip.

Married woman

High-ranking warrior

Farmer

Young girl

19

TRADE AND TAXES

Nowhere was the great wealth and power of the Aztecs better displayed than at the big city markets. Here the professional merchants, called *pochteca*, sold a variety of luxury goods—such as jade, exotic bird

Aztec "money": copper ax head, cocoa beans, and feathers

feathers, tortoise shells, and precious furs. The *pochteca* ranked one class level below the nobility. They had their own area of the cities and their own customs and gods.

Instead of using money, the Aztecs bartered for the goods they wanted, swapping one thing for another. Some goods—for example gold dust and cocoa beans—had a known value and could be used like money.

Most Aztecs had to pay taxes to the state, and these were usually collected by the local *calpulli* organizations. The Aztecs demanded large tax payments, or tribute, from the lands that they ruled over. If the subjects failed to pay, the Aztecs would send in their army and demand additional tribute.

As in most towns, the main market of Tlatelolco stood close to the city's temple pyramid. The Aztecs believed that trading in the market was a sacred duty: the gods watched over the market, and would punish any wrong-doers.

Porters

Because they did not have wagons or carriages, or any large animals to carry goods, the Aztec traders used porters. Professional porters could travel for thirty or forty miles a day at a steady jogging pace, carrying loads on their backs of up to one hundred pounds fixed to wooden frames. For a large trading caravan, hundreds of porters would be employed by the *pochteca* merchants. They usually set out and returned at night. This was because the *pochteca* were always secretive about their business affairs, and they were anxious not to draw attention to their wealth.

Apart from food, people also sold mats, baskets, bricks, firewood, cooking pots, and other useful household items.

Paying tribute

Foreign cities and provinces ruled by the Aztecs had to pay vast quantities of tribute every year—usually in the food, raw materials, and manufactured goods that were special products of their region. Tribute lists—resembling huge shopping lists—were drawn up by Aztec officials. As seen in this codex page, they could include fancy cloaks, warrior's outfits, feather shields, jade beads, sacks of cocoa beans, and rubber balls. Quantities for some items were indicated by symbols: 8,000 was represented by a tasselled bag, and 400 by a feather. This list shows a feather next to each of the cloaks, meaning the Aztecs wanted 400 of each type.

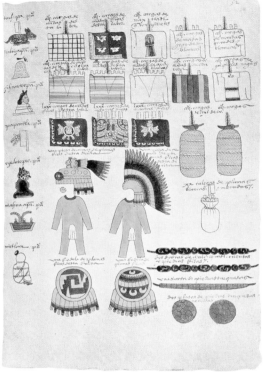

Men, women, and children came to the market to buy and sell. It has been estimated that 25,000 people visited the Tlatelolco market every day.

Leading *pochteca* merchants were in charge of the market, and acted as judges in any disputes over trade. The markets were very carefully organized and well run.

▲*The main Aztec markets were huge, and the biggest of all was in the city of Tlatelolco, which occupied the northern part of the island shared with Tenochtitlán. Many of the* pochteca *merchants lived in Tlatelolco and traded their luxury goods at the market. Ordinary citizens also came to it to sell their farm produce and their wares.*

Farmers flocked in from the countryside to sell their produce, such as melons, maize, and live animals.

POCHTECA TRADE

When they traveled abroad, the pochteca *merchants bought mainly luxury goods that the Aztecs could not get within their own empire. They traded these for works of Aztec craft—such as gold jewelry, herbal medicines, and embroidered cloth. Some* pochteca *merchants also acted as spies, collecting information that could help the Aztec rulers to decide which lands to conquer next.*

Jade beads

Pottery

Patterned cotton cloth

Pot containing honey

Jaguar skin

SCIENCE AND LEARNING

A sculpture of a man suffering from tuberculosis

Almost all Aztec children went to school, but they didn't start until they were about ten years old. The local *calpulli* ran separate schools for girls and boys, where they all learned about religion, history, counting, poetry, music, and dancing. Only the boys received military training. There were stricter, more specialized schools for the children of nobles; here they learned the skills necessary to become government officials, judges, or priests. Girls could train to be priestesses.

For the Aztecs, being able to understand what the gods intended, and what pleased them, was the greatest knowledge of all. For instance, they believed that sickness was caused directly by the gods, so the study of the science of medicine was very important. But astronomy was the most important science. It was used to calculate the calendar, which ruled every aspect of the Aztecs' lives.

The Aztecs usually made their codices from fig tree bark, which was soaked and beaten into thin sheets.

An Aztec woman preparing a medicine to treat the man's injured leg.

Medicine

To treat the sick, doctors first had to discover what had caused the illness. If they decided it was a god, special sacrifices might be required. If it was an evil spell, the doctors had to use magic. The peyote cactus was sometimes fed to the patient to produce a dreamlike state to reveal who was the source of the spell. Doctors also used medicines, mainly made from plants, such as juniper, and many of these were very effective in curing illnesses.

Peyote cactus

Juniper

The pictures were drawn in black outline and then painted in five main colors: red (cochineal), green (plant extracts), blue (flower extacts), yellow (earth), and purple (seashells).

The calendar

There were two main calendars which ran side by side. Every fifty-two years New Year's Day was the same for both. The calendar of 365 days told farmers when to plant and harvest crops. Months were marked by various rituals, such as the "volador" ceremony (right). Four men each made thirteen circuits, fifty-two in total—the number of years in the calendar cycle. The calendar of 260 days was sacred. Priests used it to tell which days were good or bad for doing certain things.

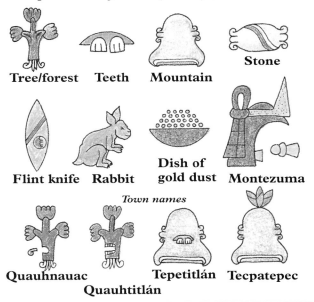

◀ *The Aztecs recorded details of everyday life in thousands of codices. They noted births and deaths, proceedings at the law courts, the tribute received by the palace from the cities and provinces of the empire, who owned what pieces of land, and so on. The Aztec system of writing was so complicated that only educated people, such as officials and priests, could read the codices properly. They employed expert scribes to make them.*

Animal skins and cactus fiber were also used to make paper.

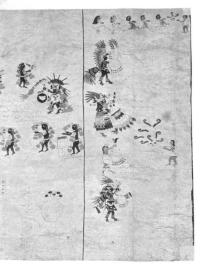

Hundreds of thousands of blank codex sheets were supplied to the Aztecs each year by foreign lands as tribute.

AZTEC WRITING

Instead of letters, the Aztecs used thousands of pictures, or "glyphs," to represent words. Glyphs were also used to represent sounds that had nothing to do with the picture itself, so the "tlan" at the end of place names might be represented by teeth (tlantli).

Tree/forest	**Teeth**	**Mountain**	**Stone**
Flint knife	**Rabbit**	**Dish of gold dust**	**Montezuma**

Town names

Quauhnauac	**Quauhtitlán**	**Tepetitlán**	**Tecpatepec**

◀*The sheets of codex books were painted on both sides and attached to each other to form a long strip. Then the pages were folded like an accordion. Some codices could be fifty feet long when fully opened up. However, very few codices have survived. This section of a sheet is from the Codex Borbonicus.*

23

WARRIORS

Aztec boys learned how to fight at school and usually had their first taste of battle as an assistant to a warrior. All men over the age of seventeen would be expected to fight in a war.

Boys learning to fight

To the Aztecs, conquering new territories was a necessity for taking over more farmland, to protect trade, to earn more tribute—but most of all to capture prisoners of war, who would be sacrificed to the gods. War was therefore a sacred duty, demanded by the gods. Priests often took part in battles.

The Aztecs were almost constantly at war. Before and after every battle, the leaders took part in long and polite negotiation and bargaining. Battles were short, and the main aim was not to kill the enemy, but to take prisoners of war, preferably without wounding them, so that they could be sacrificed later.

▲ *Pictures of Montezuma I capturing a city are carved on this stone vessel. It was used as a temple receptacle for the hearts of sacrificial victims.*

The flower wars

With some of their old enemies—notably the unconquered Tlaxcalans who lived to the east of Tenochtitlán—the Aztecs arranged ritual battles. On days specially selected by the priests, warriors faced each other on a battlefield in their full, colorful glory, which included such finery as feather-covered shields (left). Their aim was to win prisoners for sacrifice: These captives were treated with honor, and accepted death courageously, believing that they would go straight to paradise. The Aztecs called these battles "flower wars," as warriors fell like "blossom on the battlefield."

▲ *The flower wars were fought in honor of the gods. Warriors dressed for battle in the brilliantly colored costumes and headdresses which they had earned as rewards for their past successes on the battlefield. They then fought hand-to-hand, according to strict rules of combat.*

◄Leading Eagle and Jaguar knights also acted as powerful governors in the provinces. One of their ceremonial centers was a curious cave-temple at Malinalco (southwest of Tenochtitlán). The doorway is formed by a giant, carved serpent's mouth. Inside, a sculpture of an eagle with outstretched wings occupies the center of the floor, with a hole behind it for sacrificial blood. On the benches around the walls are carvings of eagles and a jaguar.

An Eagle knight

Noble warriors

The head of the army was the *tlatoani*, who had to show courage on the battlefield before he could rule. The army was run by officers drawn from the ranks of Aztec nobles. They also led the elite bands of warriors called the Eagle and Jaguar knights. These knights went into battle wearing full costumes representing jaguars and eagles, believing that this would give them the courage and strength of these animals.

WEAPONS

The main Aztec weapons were clubs and spears with razor-sharp blades made of stone. Soldiers used a spear-thrower to help them throw spears with extra force. But these weapons proved no match for the cannons and steel swords of the Spanish.

Club with obsidian blades

Spear thrower

Battle ax

Spear tipped with flint

Soldier using a spear thrower

The stone blades on the clubs were extremely sharp and able to inflict terrible wounds, or even to take a man's head off.

The bold emblems covering the wooden shields were said to have magical powers to help protect the soldier.

Off the battlefield, high-ranking Aztec warriors were entitled to wear elaborate, flowing cloaks and headdresses. But on the battlefield they wore tight-fitting outfits.

THE CONQUISTADORS

Cortés was looking for the fabled gold of the Americas

In 1492 the first Europeans led by Christopher Columbus reached the Caribbean. Within thirty years the Spanish had set up colonies in Cuba and sent expeditions to explore Central America. One of these was led by Hernán Cortés. His aim was to find gold, to convert people to Christianity, and to conquer new lands for Spain.

In 1519 Cortés marched on the Aztec capital. With the help of a large army of allies (made up of people who detested the Aztecs), this small band of Spanish conquistadors were able to defeat the Aztecs. By 1526, Cortés was the ruler of the whole Aztec empire, and the last of the ancient civilizations of Meso-America had come to an end.

Cortés' interpreter was the daughter of a chieftain from an eastern tribe. Her name was Malinalli, but the Spanish called her Doña Marina.

A god returns

The Aztecs did not know what to make of the Spanish. According to legend, in the year "one reed" (1519) the god Quetzalcoatl would return from the east to claim his throne. Some Aztecs thought Cortés might be this god. Certainly to the Aztecs, the Spanish seemed godlike, with their beards, strange sailing ships, cannons, and horses. Also, the Aztec calendar suggested the world was about to end, and there were other bad omens, such as a comet (pictured above) seen in the sky.

▲ *The Aztec emperor Montezuma II greeted Cortés outside Tenochtitlán with generous gifts. Even if Montezuma realized that Cortés was not a god, he failed to grasp that the Spanish were not like the Aztecs: The Spanish had no respect for the gods which the Aztecs so feared. They soon made Montezuma a prisoner in his own city.*

By the time Cortés reached Tenochtitlán he had just 350 Spanish troops with him. He had left the coast with 400, but fifty had died from sickness or in battles. But he also had some 4,000 allies, including Tlaxcalans and Tepanecs.

A sixteenth century painting showing the Spanish troops fighting the Aztecs.

The Aztecs had never seen horses before. They thought that the horse and rider was a two headed half-human beast.

▼ The Great Pyramid of Tenochtitlán was pulled down by the Spanish and the stone was used to build a Christian church, which was later replaced by the cathedral of Mexico City. But recent excavations have uncovered the lower part of the old temple.

The final battle

In 1520, while Cortés was away sorting out a mutiny, the Spanish in Tenochtitlán attacked the Aztecs during a festival of Huitzilopochtli. They slaughtered thousands, including many of the nobility. Cortés returned, failed to calm the situation and Montezuma was killed. The Aztecs chased the Spanish out of Tenochtitlán, killing half of them. Cortés and an army of allies then laid siege to Tenochtitlán. The city fell in 1521, and thousands of Aztecs were massacred. Cortés had triumphed.

Aztec history

The Spanish set about destroying the Aztec civilization, declaring it to be the work of the devil. But one catholic friar, Bernardino de Sahagún, decided to record as much about the Aztecs as possible before they disappeared altogether. From 1547 to 1568 he employed a team of scribes to write down all they knew about Aztec history and customs. The result was the twelve-volume Florentine Codex, now one of our main sources of information about the Aztecs.

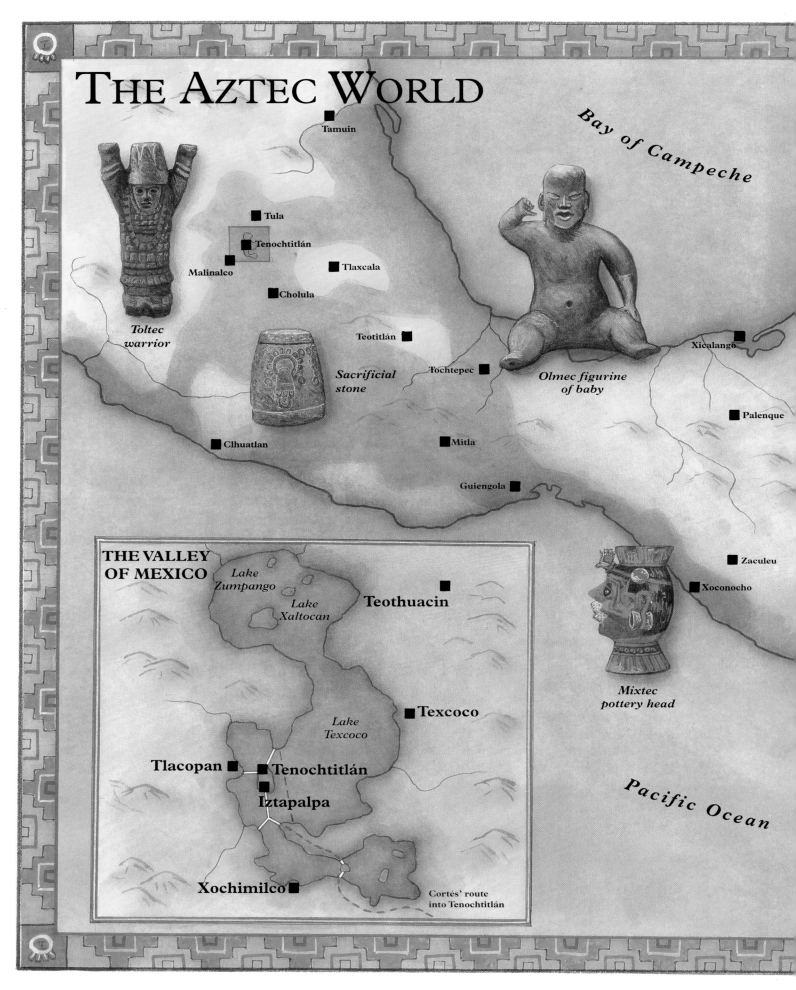

THE AZTEC WORLD

Bay of Campeche

Tamuin

Tula

Tenochtitlán

Tlaxcala

Malinalco

Cholula

Toltec warrior

Teotitlán

Xicalango

Tochtepec

Olmec figurine of baby

Sacrificial stone

Palenque

Clhuatlan

Mitla

Guiengola

Zaculeu

Xoconocho

Mixtec pottery head

THE VALLEY OF MEXICO

Lake Zumpango

Lake Xaltocan

Teothuacin

Lake Texcoco

Texcoco

Tlacopan

Tenochtitlán

Iztapalpa

Xochimilco

Cortés' route into Tenochtitlán

Pacific Ocean

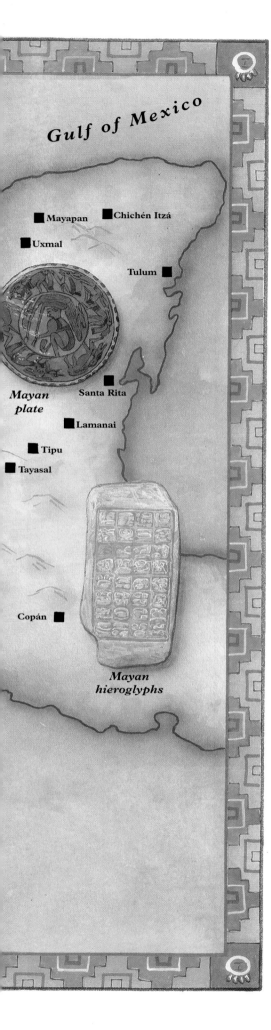

Gulf of Mexico

Mayapan ▪ Chichén Itzá ▪
Uxmal ▪
Tulum ▪
Mayan plate
Santa Rita ▪
Lamanai ▪
Tipu ▪
Tayasal ▪
Copán ▪
Mayan hieroglyphs

INDEX

A BRIEF GUIDE TO THE PRONUNCIATION OF MESO-AMERICAN WORDS AND NAMES			
Underlining indicates which part of the word should be stressed.			
Chichén Itzá	*chee-chen <u>eet</u>-sa*	Oaxaca	*wah-<u>hah</u>-kah*
chinampas	*chee-<u>nam</u>-paz*	*pochteca*	*posh-<u>tehk</u>-kah*
Coatlicue	*kwah-<u>tlee</u>-kway*	Quetzalcoatl	*ket-sal-<u>koh</u>-atl*
Coyolxauhqui	*koh-yohl-shau-kee*	Tenochtitlán	*teh-<u>nosh</u>-tee-tlahn*
Huitzilopochtli	*weets-eel-oh-<u>posh</u>-tlee*	Texcoco	*tesh-<u>koh</u>-hoh*
Mexica	*meh-<u>shee</u>-kah*	Tezcatlipoca	*tess-kah-tlee-<u>poh</u>-kah*
Nahuatl	*<u>nah</u>-watl*	Xochimilco	*show-chee-<u>meel</u>-koh*
Nezahualcoyotl	*ness-ah-wall-<u>coh</u>-yohtl*	Xipe Totec	*shee-pe <u>toh</u>-tek*

THE FINAL CONQUEST

Here is your chance to rewrite history! This is a game for two people. One player takes the role of Montezuma II, the Aztec emperor. The other is Hernán Cortés, the Spanish conqueror of Mexico. Cortés and his armies advance on the Aztec capital, Tenochtitlán. Montezuma has to fend off Cortés, and could even defeat the Spanish in their settlement. As with Cortés' victory in 1521, the outcome of this game will depend on tactics and strategy, and a bit of luck. Who will win this time? History is in your hands!

RULES

1. You will need a die or spinner (pattern provided), and fifteen counters (in three colors, five of each color).

2. Decide which player is going to be Montezuma, and who will be Cortés. Place five counters of one color on Tenochtitlán, and five on Cortés' settlement camp (the ship). Put one of each of the remaining five counters on each of the five cities (the temples eg: Jalapa.) These five counters represent other armies that can be picked up by either player during the course of the game.

3. The aim of the game is to capture your enemy's base. The first to do this is the winner. Or you can win by destroying all of your enemy's armies.

4. Players can move along the paths in any direction. If you land on a printed space, you must obey the instructions.

5. Players take turns rolling the die and moving their armies, but Cortés always starts. He moves along the path towards Tenochtitlán. He can move any number of his five counters (armies) together. For instance, if he throws a four, he can move one, two, or even all of his counters four spaces altogether in one direction. (Remember: it is best to leave at least one counter on or near your base as you may need it later to defend the base from enemy attack!)

6. Montezuma then rolls the die, and moves his counters in the same way towards Cortés' settlement. (Note: Players may wish to keep all their armies together, so they advance more quickly—or spread them out for better defense).

7. If your counter lands on a square occupied by your enemy's army (or armies), you must do battle. You throw the die again

and add the number of armies you have on that circle to the die score. Then the enemy does the same. The player with the lowest score is defeated and has to remove his army (or armies) from that square. These losing armies are removed from the game. If both players throw the same score, the battle is a draw and both armies survive. If a player loses his last army, the game ends there, and the other player is the winner.

8. Both players have the option to try to win extra armies to help them in their fight against their enemy. To do this, the player must land on one of the five cities (temples) where the other armies are based. A battle can then take place. The player throws the die. If he gets an even number he gains an extra army. If he gets an odd number he loses, and his army (armies) are removed from the game.

9. A player can capture the enemy base by landing an army on it. To do this he must throw the right number with the die. If he throws a score that is too high, he must pass through the base, to use up the entire score, then try again on his next turn. If he lands on the base and it is empty, he has won the game. If he lands on the base when his enemy has an army on it, he must play the final battle. Each player throws the die again. If the attacker has a higher score, he wins the game. If the defender wins, the attacker loses his army or armies, and the game continues.

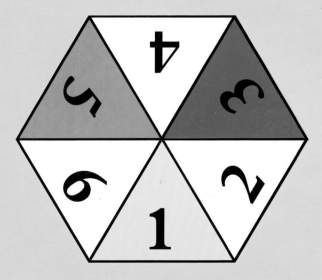

Copy the template onto a piece of thin cardboard. Cut it out and make a hole in the center. Push a toothpick through the hole and your spinner is ready to use.